Lulu Frost is the pen name of Angela McAllister, who has written over sixty books for children of all ages, including several award winners. She lives in an old cottage in Hampshire, England, with her family—her very best friends!

Lorna Brown studied fine art painting in college and works as an artist and illustrator from her cottage in Somerset, England. Lorna also works as an animal therapist, so she has the perfect balance between art, her love of animals, and the outdoors!

First published by Parragon in 2012
Parragon
Chartist House
15–17 Trim Street
Bath BA1 1HA, UK
www.parragon.com

Please retain this information for future reference.

Written by Lulu Frost
Edited by Laura Baker

Illustrated by Lorna Brown
Production by Jonathan Wakeham

ISBN 978-1-4454-9893-5
Printed in China

The Very Best Friends

PaRragon

Bath · New York · Singapore · Hong Kong · Cologne · Delhi
Melbourne · Amsterdam · Johannesburg · Shenzhen

When Grace moved into her new house, she loved the sunny yard and the tall trees. She loved her pretty new bedroom with its giant window. But she missed all her friends.

"I wish we weren't so far away," she told her puppy, Jake. "I feel lonely living here."

In the corner of Grace's bedroom was a basket overflowing with colorful costumes. Grace's favorite game was dress-up, but it was no fun to play by herself.

One day, Grace was sitting in her tree house when she heard a girl's voice in the yard next door.

Grace peeped out, but all she could see were black clothes and long, tangled hair.

"Oh dear," Grace said to Jake sadly. "I like to wear pretty colors, and I'd never have messy hair. I don't think we'll ever be friends."

Next day, Grace put on her shimmery mermaid costume
and hunted for her glittery comb and mirror.
She sat outside combing her hair,
wishing for a mermaid friend.

Suddenly she noticed a hole in the fence.

Grace
peeped
through.

To her surprise, she saw a jumble of boxes and old curtains piled up on the grass, and chairs lying topsy-turvy everywhere.

"They've filled that pretty yard with trash," thought Grace. "What a messy family!"

Next day, Grace dressed
up as a queen. She put
on a beautiful gown,
her golden crown, and
pretty party
shoes.

"Gallop away!"
she told her horse.

Later that day, Mom came home with a surprise for Grace. "Something to cheer you up," she said. She handed Grace a pair of sparkling fairy wings.

"Thank you!" said Grace happily. The wings matched her favorite fairy dress.

Grace flitted and fluttered outside, but a horrible smell was coming from next door.

Grace wrinkled
up her nose.

"Ugh!" she said.
"That's disgusting!"
And she flew back
into the house.

A few days later, Grace was
playing with Jake when a
girl wandered down the path
next door. Grace liked her
pretty dress and purple shoes.

Then Grace noticed the girl
was crying.

"Hello," she
said softly.

The girl looked up in surprise. She hadn't noticed Grace through her tears. "Are you my new neighbor?" she said quietly.

Grace nodded. She couldn't believe that this was the noisy, messy girl with the tangled hair!

The girl told Grace her name was Emma.

"Why are you crying?" Grace asked Emma gently.

"I was flying around in my bumblebee costume, and the wings caught on a tree and ripped!" she said.

"Do you like playing dress-up?" asked Grace with wide eyes.

Emma nodded. "It's my favorite game!"

"It's mine too!" said Grace excitedly. "My mom just gave me some new fairy wings. You can try them as bumblebee wings, if you like."

"Thank you!" said Emma happily.

Grace and Emma spent all afternoon playing dress-up. First Grace was a butterfly and Emma was a bumblebee.

Then Grace was a mermaid ...

and Emma
was a pirate.

Even Jake dressed up.
He barked and wagged
his tail proudly.

Next day, Emma knocked on Grace's door.
She was wearing a fairy godmother costume.
"Thank you for letting me use your fairy
wings," she said.

"Thank you for playing with me!" said Grace.
"I didn't have any friends when I moved here,
but now I have you. Aren't we lucky that we
both like playing dress-up!"

"I've brought my magic wand to grant you a wish," said Emma. "What do you wish for?"

"That's easy," said Grace. "I wish that we will always be best friends."

Emma waved her
magic wand ...

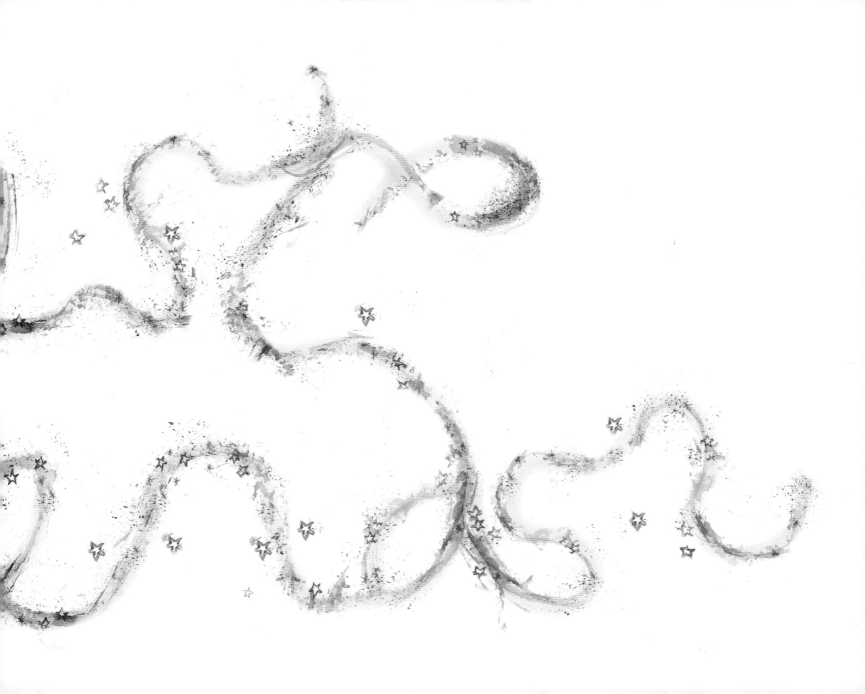

... and put a little box
into Grace's hand. Grace
opened the box. Inside
were two beautiful charms.

"Look," said Emma, "two
hearts that fit together
perfectly, just like us!"

"This is a real wish come
true!" said Grace "Let's
not just be best friends—
let's be the very best
friends ever!"